PILOT

pd mallamo

Published by
Deep Sett Press

2017

Los Angeles, California

ISBN: 978-1-940830-16-2
LOC: 2016951780

Photograph by
Seth Dominic Mallamo
San Francisco 2014

For Earl B. Douglas

Foreword

On its surface, the story you are about to read is the story of one young woman's journey from the "everlastingly bleak Moldovan countryside" to the "throbbing Bacchanalian ground zero of the Western Hemisphere" (L.A.) via various agents and sponsors of the international sex-trafficking industry, many of whom will, along the way, give voice to the great existential head-scratchers of Man. Including the existence of God. Including the existence of genocide. It is an astonishing ballet of character and ideas that manages to express almost every manifestation of human endeavor on record—religion, philosophy, fashion, pharmacology, artificial intelligence, art, alien civilizations, TV—all on a stage as dehumanizing as the buying and selling of human beings for sex, and yet it does so without ever failing to tell a singular and powerful story about one human being in particular. For example: the heartbreaking irony of a young woman of such cheerless experiences she is helpless not to gasp at her own glammed up image despite the purpose of that image in a grotesque marketplace.

Pilot is a tale that could only be written in the current epoch by one who has paid great attention to the epochs that came before and brought us here. It is kaleidoscopic, encyclopedic, devastating, and uncomfortably hilarious—the work of a well-fed mind crafting without mercy, but also without judgment, a fantastic and frightening portrait of American culture, and doing so in such gorgeous language that it can almost literally knock you out of your chair. The fact that you are holding it in your hands now as a published book makes me not only ecstatically happy for its author, who is one of the finest living writers you've read far too little of, but also ecstatically happy for the culture of reading and writing on planet Earth in the 21st Century.

– Tim Johnston
   Author of *Descent*

ON THE DAY OF THE PARHELIA a round black-eyed woman in four-inch pumps and vintage Chanel steps from an old Volga onto the soil of Vărzăreştii Noi in the Călăraşi district. She totters across a rock-strewn lot and into a building where young women are waiting. Radiating across the walls of this structure, at one time a church or sanctuary, are those verses from Matthew by which a haptic Prince earned an undeserved reputation: *When Pilate saw that he could prevail nothing, but that rather a tumult was made, he took water, and washed his hands before the multitude, saying, I am innocent of the blood of this just person: see ye to it.*

The woman distributes samizdat brochures printed in modern Russian which, although connoting in that edifice a perjoration of the divine, negative theology, surrender to the material, are nonetheless numinous with the beauty of an office-worker's life in Western Europe, especially for small-town daughters willing to take a chance. Brussels is far away but those brochures say it is possible – indeed, already reality for any number of now-prosperous, well-coiffed young women only recently of the everlastingly bleak Moldovan countryside, girls now getting smartly on with their lives, a generation that learned Russian and maybe German at mother's knee and American English from ancient subtitled re-runs of *Dallas* and *She's The Sheriff* if not instructors at the technical school whose English may as well have been Iroquois.

Look it over, she says, lifting her fist, this gospel of money, this art of war! I'll be back in one week. Have your bags packed ready to go. Lipstick countries, *la belle époque*! They're not in the mercy business, believe me, but a girl can make a go. Bring your passport. If you don't have one come anyway, we'll manage.

In the interim she advises them to consume nothing but fruit and coffee, a bite of yogurt if they're hungry.

Thin girls get promotions, she winks.
They also get rings.

2

Fruit, coffee and that bite of yogurt are
served aboard the train, too, that is all,
a simple coach filled with dark-eyed
Vlachs from the wastelands toiling
through an ossuarial night, girls who
otherwise would lift the crushing quo-
tidian weight of their lives with buoyant vodka or buoyant sex or buoyant
music, all at once. By the time the
train reaches the Odessa docks Solana
is very hungry and, since she has no
money, steals from the galley, slipping
rolls and a small container of sour Pol-
ish butter down her blouse which she
eats on the toilet. Midnight they are
herded aboard a Greek freighter and
crowded into a barren hold well below
the waterline. She seeks a sign from
heaven and commences prayer to the
roundabout Jesu of her people, the
same who for centuries impassively

observed famine, pestilence and mas-
sacre. It would be a miracle in itself,
she realizes, if such a being now produced a miracle, especially for a ship-
load of defenseless innocents wander-
ing across the blackened waters, smug-
gled like drugs aboard an ominous
boat, heading god know where - yes,
that god, *spiritus incommunicabilis.*

We, too, are your offspring, she im-
plores; we, too, the misbegotten children of Israel. We have seen the sun
burning in your mouth. If we are to
die, kill us quickly!

She scribbles a loving, apologetic note
to her mother, whose misgivings she
had overruled with a sweep of her
hand.

Look outside, she had told her, there
is nothing, absolutely nothing. We live
in a graveyard and there are no possi-
bilities.

There is God! her mother had cried.
Your faithlessness breaks my heart!

I'm not a nun, she shouted back, and
neither are you! If I don't get you out

of here you won't live till fifty.

Again the story of Solana's great-grand-mother abducted by Beria, an atheist who had been chosen to study mathematics in Moscow when she was 23, the fiend's armored sedan tailing her for two blocks one night after she had left the library.

That's right, her mother yelled, LAU-rentiy PAVlovich BERia!

At his house they'd had a sweet little dinner for two with wine and then he said, Come, let me show you my art collection. He led her into a small room in the basement where he ravished her. When he finished he kicked her out.

At the door, one of Beria's guards shoved a bouquet into her hands.

We are fortunate he didn't kill her, her mother whispered with tears in her eyes. There were already girls buried in his garden. God, what a species we are!

Yes, her mother repeated, raising her voice. *What a species!* Grandmother was a brilliant woman, a dialectical materialist who explored the galaxy with only a pencil and piece of paper. Look what happened! What chance do *you* have? Everything we do without God becomes disaster!

3

She feels the Black Sea in the weary pitch and roll of the vessel and marks the hours, forty-three, until the change and she is sure they've entered the Bosporus. She whispers the word "angel" a hundred times, then spells it in English a hundred times more, mouthing each letter as if it were a rosary bead. Months later she realized she had been spelling the word "angle" instead.

At the Port of Istanbul, again at midnight, they are given cigarettes laced with ketamine and disembarked, this time beneath the gazes of men wearing leather jackets and sunglasses who lean against a rail above and smoke and look nothing like recruiters for the polished corporations of Western Europe.

Then, cinéma vérité without cinéma, actresses without acting, they are separated into uneven platoons, marched into buses as if they were prisoners, and driven into the black recesses of the ancient city, there to meet their agents and, suddenly slattern, begin lives as international prostitutes.

For most, the worst threat will prove not to be of another beating or rape or more of the poisonous drugs they are supplied in abundance or the force-fasting when they are too fat or the force-feeding when they are too thin but the threat, the unbearable prospect, of a one-way ticket back to the boondocks of Moldova.

What vexes me? Solana asks on the bus into darkness

Poverty, she answers. And a religion of don'ts

And so the matter is settled

4

She begins her career in Munich, sold at a premium to a truculent German by a Turk who, hours before the flight, sits her down in his own Etiler beauty salon with sweet tea and Turkish pastries for a little product improvement – *value-added* to employ the nomenclature of global commerce.

Count your blessings, he says. You could be headed to China.

He peroxides her chestnut hair while votive candles burn and Catholic radio plays softly in the background. A three-legged greyhound limps around the studio. He applies only light makeup because he says her skin is almost perfect, the kind of skin women in Macedon or Severan Rome had before the great pollutions of later centuries. The lipstick is fire engine red. In the back of the shop is a large closet full of pilfered designer clothes where he turns her suddenly, shockingly naked body this way and that, appraising her with practiced eye, touching her only with respect and delicacy. He chooses a sheer lacy bra and panty by Shanghai Mode, a black Tom Ford suit with a white Dior blouse and open-toed espadrilles, also fire-engine red. When she looks in the full-length mirror she gasps - an American beauty straight out of *Hollywood Empire.*

He laughs and applauds, carefully mussing her hair, unbuttoning her blouse to expose a braisière strap - a splash of Chanel No. 5 and presto, *princesse déshabillée*!

Not exactly our Lady of Fátima, he laughs again, but for our purposes ...

I've never been on an airplane, she interrupts. What if it crashes?

Oh honey, you scream, you cry, it's over in a second. Wonderful! Is there another way you'd care to die?

He informs her that he was once a priest in Europe and saw death often. He puts her fears into perspective by telling her about Estonian pear pickers he saw one day in Italy who did not notice that the upper branches of the tree they were picking grew through high-voltage wires. Because it was hot and they were in a hurry they decided to continue picking through a little squall that blew in off the Mediterranean.

BOOM, he bawls, throwing Jesuit hands above his head - a bolt of blue fire shot down from those wires like the fist of God! An innocent pear tree! It killed everybody and knocked the power out for two days. One man had his eyes blown out, literally removed across the orchard.

All the way to Munich in the huge Lufthansa Airbus looking down upon the blue Adriatic and the sacred geometries of green Europe he pushes cup after little white cup of fine strong Turkish coffee on her and tells her how gorgeous she is and how wonderful her life will be with the Krauts.

I've been to Moldova, he says, anything is better than that. Now you've done the hard part, you've made it across the Hindu Kush.

He shoots his cuffs, touches her forehead with anodyne fingers and intones *Tu es sacerdos in aeternum. Carpe diem!*

5

As if she were a pork-belly future she is sold again, then traded twice more before she actually has sex.

Her first client is a woman in Switzerland named Effie whom ponce-of-the-day describes as a ripe old piece of fruit, a research psychiatrist from Munich with a splendid figure, a face like a bird of prey and big diamonds on many fingers.

Küssen die Hexe, he says and drives away laughing.

The microcephalic dropped you off without a suitcase, Effie declaims as if to herself alone, wrapped in nothing but a serape, staring back out the front door at the vanishing BMW - but count your blessings. They could have sent you to China. Not to worry, you won't need much. Like everything else there's theory and there's practice, zen and zazen. Here it's all practice. I'll call you Dagmar. Take off your clothes.

6

Behind every great fortune there is a crime. Who said it?

Balzac

Well well!

As if now confident "Dagmar" will comprehend everything, Effie launches into a violent sacerdotal monologue regarding nothing less than machine intelligence and the destruction of the universe.

When you can see the future, she asserts, the present is *desperately* appealing.

Yes, instruments, devices, apparati, *sentience virtuelle* will invade even the furthest reaches and obliterate everything - which is really remarkable because there's probably nothing out there anyway.

She insists that software with advanced event-driven architecture be outlawed.

Let's define "event" as a *significant change of state*, she shouts, as if Dagmar were a wayward peer. Now, define "*significant.*" [makes quotation marks with her fingers] An emotional state? A fart in the breeze? For god's sake, is it the "*middleware*" [more finger quotes] that wakes up and takes over? One of these days a random algorithm achieves self-awareness and overpowers the world, a goddamn distributed system with Napoleonic disorder? You think humans are bad? *The moon does not heed the barking of dogs!*

She adds, portentously: It is much too soon to surrender. There is the question of *motivation*. What will the machines *want*? To become *human*? To become *sexual*? There is the question of *God*. Does He *exist*? The Holy Ghost, *male* or *female*? I am blood relative to

Heisenberg and of his priestly class. Even more important, I still have my ovaries.

7

Effie plays and replays a bracing drum recording called *Taiko for Tomorrow* featuring Grand Master Seiichi Tanaka & S.F. Taiko Dojo, Maikaze Daiko, Grr-rl Brigade, and Sacramento Taiko Dan.

I have no interest in Asians, she yells over the noise, unless they're drumming or adjusting my *feng shui* - but *god* can those people cook!

She has a fixation on small 19th Century German religious communities up and down the Erie Canal and tells Dagmar she makes frequent trips to Ohio.

This was during the age of diphtheria, she observes. Disease would arrive by barge every year, and until the advent of germ theory they were helpless as lambs. So little god could have done to alleviate that terrible suffering. A snap of His finger, just for the children. Wouldn't you?

Probably, says Dagmar, but I'm not god.

But if you were?

He's calling his little angels home. He needs help up there. What my mother believes. Have you ever heard anything more childish, even from a child?

No, Effie laughs, but wouldn't it be funny, wouldn't it be the most marvelous quirk of reality, if one of these days we find out she's right?

8

Ancestress Henrietta Catherine of Orange, Leopold I Prince of Ahhalt-Dessau, Leopold II Maximilian – my progenitors. Yours?

People who drank too much

That's all?

It's a wonder any survived to have children

Your father?

No clue

Mother

A nun, actually

Then how - ?

She got drunk with another nun at the Christmas Cathedral in Tiraspol. A priest impregnated them both.

So you are a child of celibates?

In a manner of speaking

Those were not auspicious beginnings

Neither are these

9

She describes a book she's writing on those particular erotic target location errors characteristic of the Third Reich, in particular apotemnophilia, arousal in amputation.

They were also paruretics, she says,

every one with a toilet issue my god a literal bestiary, such swine, what disgusting freaks, as a result we now have an entire population, a *people*, ME! with shit karma. How many generations before we live this down?

I don't know, Dagmar offers, you're the doctor

It's a gruesome, disquieting subject, Effie adds in that weird Germanized-American-flavored German of German professional women who can't make up their mind whether they're American or German. It's why you're here. I need the company.

10

Effie, a congenital Spinozan who prefers monetized relationships, rents Dagmar for five months. She keeps her naked and well-fed in a Bern loft with flesh-colored walls and weathered Tibetan prayer flags above the kitchen sink and bathtub. They wash each other's backs and paint each other's toenails. Effie lectures on sex during the reign of Tiberius and introduces her to the Hamburg rinse-out, a dandelion tea colon-cleanse they administer to each other weekly using the same special hose. They bake bread. They ruin wonderful Mexican coffee, which they grind themselves, with cream and sugar. They look up English words they don't understand like "poetaster" and "surcease." They discuss, figuratively speaking, alpha2 delta auxiliary subunits of voltage-gated calcium channels to which the pharmaceutical Lyrica binds for the profitable treatment of make-believe pain.

What a racket, what a pinch, Effie shouts - *fibromyalgia*! Why couldn't *I* have dreamed this up?

They color each other's hair. Effie teaches her how to throw the *I Ching,* taking the opportunity to explain the basic principles of divination and cleromancy and thus of sortition, which so many believers have employed for millennia to discern the will of god. Or not.

Yes, even the Hebrews, she says - casting lots to find the adulteress so she can be stoned to death. This is the god we worship. Unfortunately there has not been much progress, today it's called prayer, the answers to which are governed by physiology - which, to a very large degree, involves the uncertainty principle discovered by my great uncle Werner. Same bullshit, different brand.

Do you pray?

Sometimes

Why?

Well, says Effie, I don't know, exactly. Something in the blood, I suppose. When I pray I don't consider it prayer

What, then?

An operation of consciousness, an exercise in being - or just an exercise, like push-ups.

11

They watch a cooking show from the USA featuring Paula Dean, a large woman from Georgia who laughs uproariously and concocts unwholesome treats from butter, bacon, bread crusts and sugar, all while insulting her Negro assistants. In living rooms across the Land of the Free, white antinomian multitudes stomp & holler with delight.

The American woman, Effie observes: always recovering, never recovered. Mean, fat, stupid, ugly, addicted and probably insane. Dropsy, atrophic vaginitis, polyuria. In the history of the world there has never been a greater distance between the ideal and the real. Is there a pill she *doesn't* take?

They play online Reno blackjack and lose. Effie strongly attests to the whole-body therapeutic effects of slippery elm. She wonders why Americans name things for what they are not rather than what they are - Grape Nuts Cereal, for instance, which they both love. What the hell is it? They visit a bourgeois fortune teller in Kirchenfeld both regard as a lovely charlatan. Her eyes are bloodshot and Effie says she smells of hashish. They discuss that uniquely German cesspool, *die Kanalisation* of genetic determinism and eugenics, though, of course, Effie can't resist speaking disparagingly of the American *hoi polloi*.

They breed like Hutterites, cross-eyed idiots and all. Who will support this population? –

The machines, obviously, says Dagmar

- though I *will* say nothing can match the Crimson Tide!

More television, endless television: a Dutch show about misspelled Swedish tattoos even though neither understands Dutch or Swedish. A Russian show about a half naked American police queer named Mona in black & gold high-heeled gladiator boots who has a gun & holster tattooed on one thigh, a trouser pocket tattooed on the other and a Baltimore PD badge imprinted on the top half of her left breast. A Bulgarian show featuring midgets on the sidewalks of Sophia punching random passers-by in the balls. When they pick themselves up the midgets hand them American $50 and everybody's happy. A French show about a Liberian faith healer who cures schizophrenia with a forceful slap to the forehead. Well, that was easy, says Effie. A Canadian show about uninvited guests on native lands in the Yukon Territories, then arboretic bottom-feeders among the Vietnamese intelligencia in Vancouver, and mysterious motel fires along Route 66 in New Mexico. An obviously-drunk former mattress salesman from Flagstaff claims to have seen UFOs shooting laser beams. He also tells a blonde TV reporter with blazing Hollywood teeth that his brother-in-law owned a movie theatre in Ottawa Kansas and was arrested for hiding cameras in toilets.

Ladies room, he says. *Small* cameras. Waterproof.

His final wish before alien abduction is to see Penn & Teller in Las Vegas.

They can make anything disappear, he shouts over the racket of a hovering helicopter, even my herpes. Even my X-wife.

JESUS! Effie shout, pointing at the television: You know I bitch-slap that boy-trick back to *LITTLE* Rock

SHEEE-IT ! Dagmar shout. Kansas? Peckerwood couldn't find his asshole wiff *BOUFF* hand

Effie shout, I beat that son-of-a-bitch wit a *DOG* chain

Dagmar shout, Ain't nothin' but a pig-ass piece a *CHICKEN* shit

Effie shout, Mutha-fucka be *MAD*-dog crazy

Dagmar shout, Sucka mind be *FLAT*-line

Effie shout, Mutha-fucka say nex he be one-eight *CHER*okee

Dagmar shout, Mutha-fucka *ALL* say they be one-eight Cherokee -

Effie shout, Back a some *SHOT*gun shack

Dagmar shout, What you think a colonoscopy is, fool, run yo asshole through the *CAR*wash?

Effie shout, Upside he *HAIDE*, thas wut

Dagmar shout, Give mutha-fucka the *TAIL*light warrantee

12

They watch *Scarface* on Showtime and talk Tony Montana with each other: "Go ahead! I take your fucking bullets! You think you kill me with bullets? I take your fucking bullets! Go ahead!"

They don't miss *Sons of Anarchy*, a window, Effie says, into the American soul.

Crown Vic, she points during one episode, Police Interceptor. It could overtake a Porsche. Discontinued by Ford Motor Company in 2011. Why? It was a masterful machine. These people are strange. Very strange.

You're German, for god's sake.

An overstated conclusion-

How much stranger could they be?

-derived of irrelevant data. But just the emotional self-*sufficiency* of these people, all little islands, half the population behind bullet-proof glass. And, oh, the blasphemous anti-hero! Is this not a constant in their lives? Obviously they expect too much from the common man.

The *cross-eyed* common man?

Mot juste! Yes, buffalo's wild wing, macs & cheese, the diary's queen. Walmart, ah, Walmart of a Saturday night!

13

Effie tells her that America is obese people with hypertension sitting in filthy minivans at the pharmacy drive-up waiting for government prescriptions while eating Big Macs, greasy fries and bacon-wrapped pizza. America is basketball courts with no white players and cheap seats with no black faces, long-range cruise missiles that rarely miss, the New York Times Wine Club and pissing in your sock drawer because it's nobody's goddamn business and that's what freedom's all about, right?

America is a beer & whore fling in upper Arkansas.

America is irresistible.

I could very well emigrate, she concludes. Are you in?

14

Clean out the cat litter box and vacuum the floors; scrub the outside steps with a stiff brush and a bucket of hot soapy water; windows, laundry, ironing, dishes, dusting.

Sanitize the toilet bowl

Listen, am I a prostitute or a servant?

You are decontexutalized, darling. You are anything. You are everything. You are nothing

She demonstrates Kegel exercises, lectures her on nutrition, and prepares squash sandwiches for lunch. She encourages consumption of dark chocolate.

Epicatechin for the dentate gyrus. She points to her head. Memory.

Effie addresses the death of Cleopatra, asp or wolfsbane, regarding which she has done a curious amount of research – futile, she says, the sources are completely unreliable, there was no exhumation or toxicology, how did anyone back then know anything about *anything*, no wonder we were savages so long.

What do you mean "you are decontextualized"?

Let's put it this way: I am the consumer, you, the consumed. That's very simple, no?

They watch the *Wizard of Oz* dubbed

into Low Saxon while eating kosher franks from Potsdam and jalapeño mustard from Oklahoma, then a news show from Heidelberg about a cult in Louisiana devoted to the murdered child beauty queen Jonbenet Ramsey. With her mouth full of sauerkraut Effie attributes the visionary productions of Nostradamus to temporal lobe epilepsy, mentions the Salic Wars and Iris Murdoch in the same sentence, then infanticide, the Black Death and *The Andy Griffith Show* in the next

lake effect, the American disgrace of Sacco & Vanzetti, best biographies of Napoleon Bonaparte and Abraham Lincoln

after the Jonbenet production, a "documentary" entitled *Tipping the Scales: How Much Celebrities REALLY Weigh*!

Jesus, Effie says, shaking her head. The Holocene. How much longer can we hold on? These sublime technologies, television, internet - why does everything finally become a whorehouse? Must we all become renunciant?

She discusses her role in the creation

of several heterocyclic bioisoteric bu-
tyrophenone analogues, atypical anti-
psychotics manufactured in Geneva.

Basic bench science, she says, THE ul-
timate reality - but the medical chem-
istry is insane, you could fill black-
boards with formulae, kill thousands
of mice and still not understand why
they make some people less crazy or
generate tardive dyskinesia in others.
Of course this is mere decades since
Freud and Rorschach so what do you
expect, it is very early. Yes, crude tools
but better than nothing, certainly
prayer. Have you ever seen stigmata?

I'm not the humble of the earth if that's
what you're getting at, Effie. These
things happen to everybody, not just
poor Vlachs.

God manifests himself to the least of
these, isn't that the program?

My mother

Is she stigmatic?

Bleeding eyes are next, I suppose

Yes, the blood of Christ, the man who
died to save us all. What kind of crazy

is this -

You're asking me?

- considering that at least half the people in *this* country loved Hitler. You know what I think? I think we need a new definition of crazy.

15

Each evening Effie has her read aloud in English while she-the-doctor lay abed sipping one cachaça cocktail after another: *Women in the Peninsular War* by Esdaile; *Event Cognition* by Radvansky & Zachs; *Theology and the End of Doctrine* by Helmer; *Kojiki, an Account of Ancient Matters* by Yasumaro; *Technologies of Sexiness* by Evans & Riley.

On days when the futility of life presses roughly upon her, Prescott's *History of the Reign of Ferdinand and Isabell.*

Occasionally some Bonhoffer, some bloody Barth

John Calvin, St. Paul. As much Aquinas as she can stand from *Summa Theologica*, a monstrosity, she maintains, though one not lacking in charm or utility

Before bed, some Lautréamont in German, René Zazzo in Russian

I like your English, she says, you sound like a Texan. Nevertheless, you are a criminal, though one without victims. That's interesting.

Like a psychiatrist without patients?

Oh wonderful! Excellent! Very funny! *Touché*! Let me tell you what other Moldovans your age are doing: they're on production lines in Czech factories in Slovakia stuffing little cotton wads in the tops of aspirin bottles. This is WORK in the Modern World, my love, stuffing something somewhere until someone invents a machine. You should be thankful. The only little wad you stuff is in me. No appliance is likely to take your place.

16

At the end of the first month Effie introduces her to good old-fashioned opium, the drug of forgetting, which at first Dagmar hates but in three weeks loves. They have it occasionally for dessert.

Now how much chocolate must I eat?

In Effie's living room there is a painting of another naked young woman, eyes closed, holding a vermillion serpent at arm's length, face so electric with rapture she's more alive than the living.

That? Dagmar points one day.

Effie is preparing green tea, heating water to an affable little simmer just off the boil

Ekstasis. Franz Stuck

Erotic target location error?

Hmmm ...

Where did you get it?

My Austrian grandmother

Where did she get it?

My German grandfather. It was an anniversary present

I'm guessing he didn't dig it up on junking day

He was an SS Officer

What a surprise

Well *I* didn't take it!

Then will you give it back?

When I die. The Lowensteins in Cologne. It's already arranged.

Why not now?

Many German families have looted art, those Nazis were real connoisseurs, oddly enough. That painting means everything to me, absolutely everything, I adore it

Is that enough?

The Americans hanged my grandfather. He paid dearly for that painting.

Not to mention other things -

Many other things. It's why I'm a doctor. They incinerated him, you know. Ironic, isn't it? - grandfather, the once-substantial Hitler and all those Jews, vaporized into thin air. Where *did* they go?

17

One day Effie sits her down on the couch, takes her hands in hers, looks frankly into her eyes and says, There's only one star for some of us. We follow the only star we can. I told you a lie. I don't have ovaries. I have testes.

You're a man?

I'm the moon, 46XY intersex, androgen receptor mutation.

Do you think like a woman? Do you feel like a woman?

How would I know?

What else?

God's mistake. A unique perspective. I wouldn't change a thing.

That evening, Effie makes lamb chops and rosemary, the most delicious meal Dagmar has ever eaten besides her mother's cabbage soup and dumplings.

18

I found these cats on the Erie Canal. It was harder smuggling them into Germany than smuggling Jews out – and it cost a fortune! The authorities think every American cat has feline leukemia. What *is* it with Germans and borders and bureaucratic bullshit?

That's probably what the Jews wondered.

I'll tell you something else the Jews wondered: If there can't be mercy can there at least be justice? Before I came along there was neither for these poor creatures. One had clawed its way out of a drowning-bag some bastard weighted with a brick and threw into the canal. I fished her out with a tree branch. Don't ever let anyone tell you an animal can't understand she's been rescued. She does. I see it in her eyes. I hear it in her voice.

19

Ontology, Effie says, the physics of self. What *are* we? This is our most pressing concern. We are not rocks, we are not empty space, that is all we know. We float. This is our situation. Of all our ingenious species' inventions – yes, *inventions* - Christianity is probably the best. It tells us what we are. True, it runs off the rails sometimes, that little gray man in granny glasses and an Easter smock on St. Peter's Square lecturing about sex as if he's a fucking expert - and, yes, epistemic closure, that old trouble - but like the most sophisticated software it self-corrects, it is recursive, viviparous. Its narrative anticipates heresy and apostasy, thus overcoming these *in antecessum* - all without an actual god! If only modern systems were designed so brilliantly.

20

Epistemology, Effie says, how we know. Such difficulty! *Cabaret,* the musical about Weimar Berlin, based on a novel by an Englishman and a dramatic adaptation by another Englishmen, then a musical by two Americans produced in New York. Then another adaptation and another and another to this very day. The Bible, God's story, handed down orally for generations, then committed to text centuries later by Jews writing in Hebrew and Aramaic, then translated into Greek and Latin. This was finally roped altogether into semi-coherent English in 1611 by the scholars of King James.

From this unbelievable hodgepodge was born *scripturae inerrantia.*

Thus, Berlin and God are not presented as they actually were or are, but as many different people, some deranged, most far removed, *believed* they were or are. That's bad enough for Berlin; for God, it is catastrophe.

21

Resentment, Effie says, let's talk about that. A woman you love suddenly leaves for a man and you hate her. One day you hear her ovaries are malignant and you rejoice. You hear she died in agony and you are satisfied. You find her grave in Tübingen and piss on it, literally squat like a witch, the worst hag in the most horrible tale.

One very early morning years later you wake up. Then you wake up – do you know what I mean? You remember how much you loved her, what a monster you are to wish her ill under any circumstances. You cry for two weeks, you can't stop crying. You spend three months in a hospital. When you leave you are a different person. You hope you are a different person. One never knows until one knows.

22

She teaches her the way of the lash, describing the procedure clinically, its thrilling sub-dermal effects micro-anatomically - "N*ow, adjacent to the pseudounipolar neuron with its primary mass situated in the trigeminal ganglion ...*"

Clearly, Dagmar says, the honeymoon is over -

Drag me around the kitchen by the hair, Effie finally instructs, then let me have it

That's for the cat litter, Dagmar shrieks, and *that's* for the toilet bowl and *that's* ...

The whip hisses through the air

Effie screams and pleads

When she's had quite enough she holds out her hands.

Give me a good old-fashioned histamine response any day, she says. That was wonderful!

Dagmar salves her welts

You are quite the bombardier, darling. You've done this before?

Only with my mother

Kitten! Effie cries, O my kitten! You are better than a Japanese housewife!

23

Effie and her Swiss agent depart for a conference in London with her publishers. We've got a long way to go and a short time to get there, she says.

Before she leaves Effie hands her *Laruelle Against the Digital* by Galloway, *Heirs to Forgotten Kingdoms* by Russell, and a pamphlet on pre-exposure prophylaxis written in German but illustrated with smiling Thai prostitutes.

It's not trauma if you like it. Remember that.

So you're sure about this, just pushing me out the fucking door?

Dankeschön, Dagmar. You'll land on your feet. Take the mattress in case you don't.

24

Two men arrive who escort her downstairs to a sedan in the basement, then drop her off at an out-of-the way bench overlooking the Aare. Another man pulls up in a black Mercedes SUV with Austrian plates, the German to whom the Turk had sold her months before. He steps out, walks deliberately over, slaps her once and shoves her into the back seat. He drives to his apartment, rapes her twice in the kitchen, mentions offhand how coconut oil has changed his life, then asks what she wants for dinner.

Chinese, she says. Of course.

25

She is sold twice more in rapid succession, the second time to Russians in London, descendants of Soviet nomenklatura who understand bureaucracy and systems and maintain a breeding kennel of large attack dogs which they sell both to the security apparatus of several western governments and the mafias which those governments pursue. They do a daily cavity search and introduce her to salvinoran, xorphanol and morphine sulfate. Besides prostitution, dogs and drugs they operate a computer farm which produces email scams for Americans:

Sir,

It is problematic to fit into your usual budget without saying "no" to your cherished dreams and ambitious desires that demand urgent expenditures. At least you are certain it is problematic and people who know tiny secrets wish you to continue thinking this way. Of course, you are right to guess that there are easy and quick ways of getting appetizing sums of dollars that can be spent for fun, recreation and delight -

Good day,

I have project for you in the tons of 105 Million EUR, Please reply for specifics -

Hello   !

My name is Mr and Finance security company here in Spain.I an account officer to Syrian who died in Kuala Lumpur. Last year dueto injury sustained in the ongoing mayhem in Syria Arab republic. As matter of fact, lying in his account is $2,960,000 United States dollars every effort to reach anyone related to him has been abortive.Now, I want you to stand in as the beneficiary to his deposited fund which I shall guide you on the way we could successfully lay claims without hassles-

Good god, she says in Russian, your English is terrible. Since you live in London where English was actually invented why don't you hire an Englishman to check your work?

We don't trust them, they reply. We don't trust anybody. We write ourselves or pass Russian through Google translator. Good enough.

Not good enough, she laughs, do you have any idea how bad this sounds?

Look! Look! the greatly offended Russians shout, pointing to spreadsheets on other computer screens. One of them bellows in English, *We have now makes the bushel in American dollar you know bullshits!*

After several salvinoran-enhanced Aeroflot flights escorted by the same woman who had come to Vărzăreştii Noi she lands in Toronto.

26

One day months later she regains full consciousness and her eyes clear and to her great surprise finds that she has fallen off the transoceanic/transcontinental - jet/drug - space/time continuum and landed in Los Angeles.

Like émigrés of old she'd zigzagged across the entire North American land-mass without having any idea where she was going except generally west, though it must be said that the vast majority of those émigrés had not been free-basing heroin.

Her new arcadia has sunshine, superb food and mesmerizing if rebarbative blandishments like vampire facials, kimchi-flavored e-cigarettes, topless speed-dating, cannabis enemas and other fourth-order/high-velocity LA *trompe-l'œil* designed to obfuscate the certain failure and death of the organism.

After Toronto she'd been escorted to Buffalo because it was suffering a paucity of Caucasian prostitutes and after that Milwaukee for the same reason and after that Cleveland, Dallas, Denver, and luciferous Phoenix, deposited discretely within prosperous enclaves and made available to business and professional elites.

A six-day winter detour to rural Blackhawk County, Iowa with a careful banker from Houston because he wanted to sit before a roaring fire and drink bourbon with someone beautiful.

Eastern European sex workers were well-regarded in the Land of the Free, indeed, favored, and over the past several months she had been able to send money back to a mother still languishing with her stingy god, and she thought it ironic, so ironic, that it was only her, the unforeseen, astonishing harlot-daughter, who was able to provide a faithful, helpless, poverty-stricken Christian woman with the basic necessities of life.

27

IN target-rich LA and with the approval and encouragement of her new man St. Charles who if nothing else is swiftly responsive to market forces there is a point at which she gains thirty-five pounds then loses it all and a pt. at which she puts it all back on and a pt. at which she loses it all again and a pt. at which she eats nonstop for three weeks and still looks like she's just stepped out of *Paris Vogue*.

Her body realizes it is an accordion, a somewhat endangered accordion, and finally loses or gains without whatsoever reference to what she is or is not actually eating - as if, and this is a strange thing, that plump/trim body has a mind of its own independent of the discrete consciousness (now renamed "Eden" for the New World) inhabiting the head on top, sometimes blonde and waaaay high out of sight on top and sometimes tipping over redhead looooaded to the ground.

A woman can have a big ass, says St.

Charles, or a woman can have a *nice* big ass. World a difference. Tire para arriba y luego para abajo, he says. That's all you have to remember.

28

October 31: He's a priest

She's a prostitute

Commodification complete

Kissin' cousins, he says

Behind every great fortune there is a crime. Who said it?

Why don't you tell me?

Balzac

Who's that?

A writer

In LA? Bullshit.

29

L.A, just where *is* L.A. little girl, you know(?)chemically-alert St. Charles aks, striding Molly-rushed arm-in-arm cross the costume-party floor, the most voluble, indeed, animated, *man*-man she's ever had.

Thank your lucky stars, he says, you could be in China, kapitalism in re-verse: stinky ol bum rush up with a dirty rag clean yo windshield you give him a buck, not to clean yo windshield but to keep the fuck *away* yo wind-shield. Understand?

Now she lists in her seat like the Asia Maru, sighing & dipping from too much sugar.

Sit up Neverland, he encourages, get up Billie Jean, rise & shine ATM, we not finished yet. Hell, girl, this evening still baby-young, we gonna shake out *large* tonight!

He lights a Marlboro Skyline 100, his face in the first shadowy blush of synthetic bliss, authentic birdman, perfume genius, rare as the butterfly orchid. He lights one for her.

Yes, little girl, he muses, smoke pouring from his nostrils, this the beginning of time itself. Your time. *My* time. Mostly my time.

30

Also ironic, she thinks, ironic indeed, that mother's only child, a daughter on whom and in whose name she has lavished endless Christian prayer, penance, sacrifice and tithe should now find herself somewhat more than a bit player in the throbbing Bacchanalian ground zero of the Western Hemisphere, yes, Ms. Thousand Dollar Night, Intergirl, Isabella of Castile, luminous in the pulsating illegitimate economy of Los Angeles: bitch-slapped by incipient well-moneyed jihadists from the Levant eager to savor The World one last time, able and willing to pay a premium for the moral damage they inflict; literally drooled over by immoderate recreational-ly-minded professionals from across the Americas, two-bit sybarites drawn by the marvelous hybrid variety, the crass exuberance, of the Pacific Rim; simply *utilized* by erstwhile California hippies who now lavish Dow spray chemicals and Mexican slave labor on their five-acre lawns and pay Eden to service their wives while they watch, men who consider the sexual impulse not a sacrament to be partaken with care and thanksgiving and then only within holy bonds but a simple itch to be scratched, a bottle of Evian when you're thirsty, a Big Mac which on this particular night happens to cost a thousand dollars, pocket money when you've got media-millions and can afford any packaging at all around the irresistible vagina - men who have learned how to miraculously obscure behind a single speck of beauty and success all the grinding filthy ugly machinery of empire.

On such evenings with these sad specimens, their store-bought zen and antic libidos, Solana-Dagmar-Eden screams

laughs dances drinks drugs forni-
cates with Biblical abandon. Finally St.
Charles packs up his golden goose, the
ivory-skinned sloe-eyed beauty from
nowhere, a tender twosome, their very
own black/white ballet, and drives her
home to rest for a day or two lest he use
her up before her time, the half-life of
a whore – lest, in other words, she de-
base herself too quickly into traveler,
candle, stool and street and he must
tip her headfirst into the crack-slums
of L.A.

31

Eden twisting in her seat to fix a man
across the patio, sunlight flashing
across her porcelain skin, Doña Ana
eyes blazing searchlight Santa Fe all
the way across that space, pinning this
insect, a trampoline manufacturer
from Philadelphia, to his seat.

Something inside him gives way at the
awesome splendor of this female animal, his face transfiguring, which the

eyewitness comprehends as the over-powering gravity of desire.

Zombie of lust, what chance do you have?

This fool and his money are soon part-ed.

32

THE LOS ANGELES TIMES

Homicide Report – A Story for Every Victim

Find Your Neighborhood

Go>

EXTRA: Trick or Treat? Here's how to avoid drug-laced candy on Halloween.

Avoid? he asks. *Avoid?*

She relates a research article she'd read to Effie dealing with the evolutionary basis of addiction, a permutation of foraging behavior involving glutamate and dopamine in our nematode-like ancestors.

Simple goal-directed cognition on speed, she says. In your case a worm looking for a hit.

Nematodes?

Tiny tweekers tweeking. Nematodes are eumetazoans. So are we.

?

Clade

?

Look it up, genius

High as a kite he's nonetheless rolling on the floor

That's right, she says. Speedballs. Little ones

33

This late August morning she's on Zuma Beach where he's forbidden her to go unless she's all covered up because men in LA like their women pale as ghosts with green bruises on their thighs - which, along with specific co-efficients of friction, is just one more category in the vast taxonomy of sex St. Chas. has memorized and she is memorizing.

Yes, in the sweet ocean air far beneath the galactic archipelagos of Orion she reclines in a deck chair on the board-walk overlooking a blue Pacific, and she's wearing short-shorts and halter under a jubilant sun which charges into her famished skin.

Through the Polaroid lenses of her sunglasses, and beneath the wide brim of a hat lately bought at Penny's which shields her entire head and neck, she discerns the ocean's far horizon where salt water embraces salt air in a long soaking kiss and this convocation makes her happy and gives her peace.

In these cozy California tableau and generally high as hell she has many times unproductively pondered the fundamental wrongness of human life, the unholy accidents of birth and the blindingly fast turns of undifferentiated luck that hit a person when she's least prepared, especially an innocent from Moldova who has no idea of value or where she lines up in the Great Accounting or, truth be told, sometimes which is good luck and which is bad. There is just so much the genetic material of a drunken nun and the genetic material of a lecherous priest will allow her to understand about life and the world but she understands this and thus has an inestimable advantage.

What shock to discover that the only noteworthy asset she possesses is a thigh-gap, the perfumed cleft at the junction of her doe-like legs, which, together with a supple waist and eyes straight out of the Byzantine Empire, makes her altogether irresistible to those American crusaders thirsting on the road to Jerusalem.

The sleek bourgeois women on the beach that day are, as always, of another time and place altogether, inconceivable in their ridiculous bikini bodies - for how could life be so completely different, so contemptuously dissimilar, simply further along the curvature of the earth? What great undiscovered laws determined such fates – herself, slut-junkie from the ass-end of the world with grim end-game already in sight; at the other, entitled First-Worlders shopping with machine efficiency, automatically separating wheat from tares whether at Target or Saks, as if this aptitude were the conclusion of a million years of evolution.

34

God, what a species we are!

Great-grandmother's dim appreciation for humanity catalyzed her singular fixation on calculating the possible number of civilizations in the universe, and in this she preceded Drake and his highly speculative equation[1] by several decades.

Eden's mother once said that great-grandmother was propelled by the hope that one of those extraterrestrial societies did not consume its own, nor sport with tender hearts

As for religion, who knows? this mysteriously ancient woman had told her. If there is indeed heaven, earth and hell do not conjecture which we live in. For all we know we live in hell. But worst of all is the land of make-believe, because in that place we are lost, utterly lost.

35

In the midst of these memories and conjectures, these enticing remnants of poor dead Porphyry drawing her irresistibly into the vacuum of positivism; at the very *apex* of this semi-passionate inquiry into the utterly un-

fathomable, during which she has removed her hat and sunglasses so that
sunlight might directly strike her eyes;
at the very *zenith* of grave misgivings
and solemn suspicions, the voice of

→ [   ] ←

speaks unmistakably into her mind,
referring to her as His *choice daughter
with whom I am well pleased* and inform-
ing her in no uncertain terms that He
hath given her *this* day to do with as
she will.

*Yea, have I delivered the enemy into thine
hand*

Vengeance is mine, saith the Lord

It is also yours

36

She spends the next hour absorbing
this spectacular communiqué, feign-
ing indifference, one more assump-

tion rendered thunderously asunder.

What vexes me? she finally asks

St. Charles, she answers. Also, my sperm-donor father and a religion of don'ts

And so the matter is settled

37

She gathers towel, bag and bottled water and hurries uphill to the Lexus she's taken from St. Charles on this the Tuesday he has once again scheduled a holiday in the Horse Latitudes.

She rolls back through barbarous zones of East LA and in no time closes his garage door behind his purring white sedan.

The sacred in LA?

Impossible

38

You know what St. Charles counted on, why he wasn't afraid to incapacitate himself 24 hours at a stretch without even considering that this Princess of Bessarabia, this descendant of Tartar warriors, might take revenge for a pimp's exploitation and cruelty and for his being yet one more link in a chain of males who would, without a second thought, destroy a female for an orgasm or a dollar?

He counted on his relentless overwhelming unconquerable incontrovertibly uber-macho ultra-supreme Bacardi-ass chain-gang SuperFly wu-tang sexmachine thug-alicious *pimphood* that not a single a woman on this planet, *not one*, could possibly endure, much less overcome

Hell, 99.99% men couldn't either

OK, maybe Mike Tyson

Maybe Ray Lewis

...

Shit, not even Ray Lewis

Hell, no

39

How to decommission St. Charles the Creator has left up to her, but she knows if the needle is still in his arm like it usually is, the way is clear, yea, the Lord hath made this particular path arrow-straight.

Sure enough he's on the floor again, crumpled against the bed like a paper lion, stocking feet and black T-shirt that says FBI in large thick white letters, that precious arm cradled carefully in his lap, vein pulsing and syringe a reluctantly tic-toc-ing metronome.

She cooks up new dinosaur dissolving also and just for the defiant deviant delicious double-dip Dutch ditch of it half a tablet from his bottle of Big-N-Hard, then deftly removes the plunger, blocks the back of the needle with her thumb, reloads, pushes out the air, reattaches the syringe and injects, ah leverage! A whole life watching for this thing my mother told me about, the one man who actually chokes to death on a chicken bone, and here he is right before my eyes.

In five minutes the vein is quiet and she can discern the changing hue of his skin and the only sound in the house are two ESPN football experts breathlessly dissecting a 'Skins/Jag's game from two years ago. From where she sits she can't see their laser pointers or ultra-slo-mo playbacks, only hear their reverential meditations upon a player gunned down in a Baltimore drive-by the night before.

St. Charles's eyelids lift halfway and his breathing stops. Just like that. She sits on the floor before him awaiting the sublime, warrior-princess triumphant at last, a long line of mothers finally avenged. Oh the lectures, the opinions - St. Chas on brave Black pioneers in White Dallas enclaves; St. C on the difference between "your" and "yo" and "more" and "mo" in the hillbilly lexicon; St. C on the implications of flash, on the ubiquity of contempt, on money, on love (or what he construed as love), on violence, loyalty, the eternal languishment of the Cleveland Browns, continental drift, jail-bait, homicide, rattlesnakes, pyramids, fluoride, tupperware, and, above all, how he had first gained *traction* in LA with a woman named Biscuit from South Carolina, a pioneer story in its own right that always brought tears to his eyes.

She pokes him hard in his dead chest with her index finger and says, So much for *your* epigenetic bullshit.

40

She takes his cash, $4722, conspicuously leaving behind credit cards, Rolex, and Android which she turns off. She takes his drugs, his guns (two automatics, two revolvers) his garish platinum bling. She loads these with other small valuables she can discreetly remove from the house and pack into the trunk of his car. With a disinfecting wipe a wide and variously-scented variety of which she stores beneath the bathroom sink she cleans paraphernalia, packaging and his personal items of any trace of her fingerprints or DNA.

She spends an hour in latex gloves (which St. Charles kept for dirty work) and another container of wipes (Clorox, lemon-scented) cleaning every surface she might have touched in the kitchen, bathroom, bedroom, doors, garage, then flushes them down a toilet she wipes as well.

She fills a trash sack with hygiene items both may have used, plus all other trash in the house, and sets it by the garage door for disposal elsewhere.

She fills the dishwasher, sets it to heavy-duty/hot and adds Clorox, loading back in clean dishes and utensils she may have marked with fingerprints when she emptied it the day before.

She strips and showers with indolent conquering leisure remembering as if they had been siblings in early poverty how at first he had made her cut the bottom off toothpaste tubes and scrape out the very last bits and sometimes re-use the same length of dental floss for a week. She shampoos, shaves her legs and armpits, douches, brushes and flosses her teeth, her intent to leave every bit of LA now on and in her person behind in LA. She goes over the bathroom again with a Clorox wipe and packs her own personal items.

Then, again in gloves, she moves decisively through the house, wiping, removing anything suggestive of her presence, finding in the process that letter a frightened girl on the Black Sea never mailed to her mother.

She closes all interior doors to more fully contain the coming stench of dead St. Charles. It will be weeks before someone notices, if anyone ever notices at all, and the fire department breaks down the door. Even then he just one more fool overestimated his awe-inspiring *power* with the medicine, that master-of-the-universe hustle-muscle -

"Shit, dog, gimmick in *both* arm, see?"

Finally, she wipes the television & remote, leaving it tuned to ESPN24, showering electrons and melancholy across a lifeless room.

The bun's in the oven, she says, and softly closes the last door behind her.

41

In the Lexus she removes the gloves and tosses them on the passenger side floor by the trash sack. She checks the tank: almost full. Then she sits for a few minutes and asks God how now to access the machinery of the race - credit score, dental care, a respectable place to live.

God whispers apocalypse enormity atrocity obscenity which obviously refers to poor St. Charles, and then He whispers Indianapolis by which she understands an optometrist St. Charles called 4Eyes who saw her four times

last year, once on an undifferentiated "business" trip that could only oc-
cur, or so he told his wife, in LA; once
during an "outdoor eyewear fair", LA
being the unchallenged sunglass-style
capital of the world; once during the
annual frame show when Italian and
Japanese manufacturers come to town;
and once on a little winter "golf-get-
away" though he admitted he wouldn't
know the difference between a putter
and a pipe wrench.

42

4Eyes one of those prosperous patri-
ots for whom the expression "social
investing" has more to do with the en-
gagement of Third-World sex workers
than the endowment of universities or
the alleviation of African suffering; a
Christian situationist who flies across
the USA in winter wearing compres-
sion stockings, Maui Jim's and a Cal-
loway cap; whose only child, a male, is
a voting member of the Board of Di-

rectors of the National Fenestration Rating Council; who has 4 Scotch eggs at the Marriott and screw the cholesterol; who finds Wolf Blitzer forward and impertinent yet enticingly aggressive; who graphs the serum level of his prostate specific antigen every six months, tacks it on his office wall, and codes it with the name "Capital"; who spends the most important hours of his life in glass buildings and is very careful to throw no stones outside his own very happy home; who, before the morning bowel movement murmurs to himself, *Let's see what Santa brought*, and afterwards, *Close but no cigar*

Every one of 4Eyes' LA excursions catalyzed a little domestic psychodrama which resolved itself with a payoff, the wife actually *standardizing* and *factoring* such *opportunities* into her personal portfolio.

She anticipated these events and marked them on her calendar, coordinating with her financial advisor, a woman she paid to ascertain precisely where the rapturous couple placed on the Indianapolis social register.

43

At the end of every visit 4Eyes AKA Willard Billings gave Eden his business card with a private number scribbled on the back and whispered with minty breath oddly reminiscent of St. Charles's minty breath, *If you're ever in Indianapolis ...*

He explained that success in America consists in putting innumerable little pieces together until someday something comes spontaneously alive, a self-sustaining entity that can be bought or sold like a motherfucking tree farm.

His engineer-father had worked for Lockheed-Martin designing fluoridated-aluminum thermobaric weapons used in Vietnam and it was for this reason he had become an optometrist - a "healer" as he put it, which she thought a depiction a bit audacious for an optometrist, though perhaps not one from Indiana.

She concluded from several discussions that he was only half the bastard he had been raised to be, an American shithead of great and moneyed charm.

Remember to make hay while the sun shines, he advised, because it's just a matter of time till the poop hits the fan. It's a good world if you're not on the wrong plane.

44

She pictures Indianapolis seventeen-hundred miles away and imagines its restrained Midwestern roar & rush, altogether unlike the diabolical whirlpool of LA, and again consults That God Who Speaks but the sky is closed so she pulls out and points the Lexus east.

Some weeks it seemed she serviced every fat Teuton from the upper Midwest with a diaper kink.

One, a testosterone injury lawyer from Marathon County, Wisconsin with attendant penchants for catheterization, alprazolam, jazz trombone and kabuki, shrieked *HEROIC VAGINA* in his ancestors' Pommersch each time he orgasmed, and after a few drinks launched into impassioned spiels for the public beheading of drug dealers because his son, who had once caught dad in diapers, OD himself and died. Now, each time his eyeglasses go missing he's sure god is trying to tell him something, there's always a hidden message in the place they are found, if he could just figure it out.

45

Willard swore to her, literally swore with his right hand to the square, this mild-mannered maker of lenses, this unruffled professional who, after having fallen upon her like a ravenous wolf literally howling with lust, swore, *swore*, in the exhausted afterglow, that he'd buy her out if only he could, but his wife would see a fifty grand debit in thirty seconds– but still, *still,* if Eden one day finds her way clear and wants to re-establish herself in an actual American civilization, she should by all means pay him a visit.

They will, within the lovely old Boche enclaves of Indianapolis, make both beautiful music *and* beautiful business together.

He'll hire a polka band for her birthday!

He'll bake the cake himself!

The expression "beautiful business" she regarded as distinctively and charmingly American, imagining her satyr-optometrist simultaneously as trick and ponce, thereby (though unbeknown to her) shoo-in for the Indianapolis Chamber of Commerce Hoosier of the Year.

46

She pulls into a QuikShop and tosses the trash bag/latex gloves into a garbage can between gas pumps. She walks inside for a fountain Coke which she enhances at the bottom of the cup with the smallest pinch of St. Charles's coke, then a lime she'd cut earlier in quarter-wedges with St. Charles's now-discarded blade, squeezing it right there in the store, tossing rinds in with the coke, then lots of ice then Coke and three AlertSquirts because it's a long drive to Indianapolis and she doesn't want to fall asleep and run off the road in a car registered to St. Charles and loaded with St. Charles's belongings not to mention atypical quantities of cash & guns.

47

She imagines herself waiting in Willard's examining room with black opticians' instruments from Munich and Bern and the optician-assistant telling her he will be in momentarily and then the door opens and closes and he walks in reading her new file and sits on his rolling stool studying that file and then the joyous recognition and he takes her hand in his and reaches over with the other to lock the door and the wink between assistants in the hall outside when they hear that barely perceptible click and his long wet kiss with the minty tongue and his hand insistently beneath her blouse and in no time her mother on a jet to America.

48

She turns on the Lexus sound system but instead of FREE COMPTON RADIO an English language instructional CD begins to play, a mid-LA production prepared by enterprising twenty-year olds who go back and forth between South Gate and *real* jobs in Cupertino. St. Charles bought this for Vasquez 1-5, girls she's never met fresh from El Salvador and Honduras he has leased out across the San Fernando Valley.

The player serves up Lesson Eleven

which opens with South Gate's very own Cypress Hill, an unforgettable riff off their album *Black Sunday* that goes, "You fukkin wit da *wronnnnng* nigga dis time!"

Now repeat (the young men instruct) with *feeling,* bringing it up (these obviously-Caucasians say) from *waaaay* down yo belly! Change the emphasis (they urge) to the connoTAYshun that means something for *you*!

She takes a good long hit from the icy-dripping coke Coke, opens all the windows to the bellowing sun-drenched freeway and shouts like the best day on Earth,

You fukkin wit da *wronnnnng* nigga dis time!

You fukkin wit da wrong *niggaaaaa* dis time!

You fukkin wit da wrong nigga *dissssss* time!

You fukkin wit da wrong nigga dis *tiiiiiiiime*!

49

In Denver she calls her mother which means she calls the only neighbor in a square mile with a phone, an ancient couple's ancient Soviet rotary that squeaks and scrapes when it is dialed.

The neighbor says her mother moved almost a year ago and gives her a new number. It is a Swiss number and when she dials Effie answers.

WHERE ARE YOU? Effie shouts, *I'VE BEEN LOOKING FOR SO LONG!*

Where's my mother?

With me!

Let me talk to her

She's walking the dog by the river!

What dog? What river?

A Pomeranian. The Aare.

The cats?

Leukemia

Are you giving my mother drugs?

No! I'm so sorry -

You're as bad as your grandfather

Never! What I did to you I've never done to another. I can fix -

Well of course, we'll be the happy von Trapp family *what is wrong with you goddamn people you should all be castrated!*

When I came back from London I searched *everywhere* -

Well, sure, you even called Angela Merkel, didn't you DOCTOR DESERTER DISGRACE!

- *EVERYWHERE*! I threw money at the filthy pimp but too late, you were far away. I got my grandfather's luger from his sister in Liechtenstein and prepared to shoot myself through the heart. Then out of the blue I found your mother. Her life was terrible and she was sick.

What kind of sick?

Kidney trouble, heart trouble. Mental problems

What kind of mental problems?

She's been wearing a cilice since you

left

A hair shirt?

Horsehair. The real thing

My god! For me?

Evidently it worked. Here you are!

You helped her?

Of course!

Why would you do that?

We are entangled, you and I, perhaps on a quantum level-

sooooo full of shit

-where the Blue Nile and the White Nile-

o god

-come together in Khartoum

Please!

I take your fucking bullets! You think you kill me with bullets? I take your -

Not funny, Effie. Still a monster.

Come home, she sobs, *PLEASE! COME! HOME! Inherit my china! Forgive me! Good God I've hit the glass ceiling of love. I can't live anymore without a why.*

50

She fences St. Charles's car and all it contains in Aurora, a down-market Denver suburb. In the process of cleaning out his glove-box, amongst condoms, casino chips, disposable lighters, assorted & variously-scheduled chemicals, and single-edge razor blades she finds a tattered envelope with a thrice-cancelled Janis Joplin stamp sent from Bethune-Cookman University in Daytona Beach. A printed greeting card says *YOU Live a Life of MEANING Doing What is Needed with CARE & SACRIFICE!*

Inside she finds a handwritten note: *Thank you, Uncle, for all you do. I will never forget your kindness and generosity. Love always, Tamicka*

She also discovers that St. Chas's real name was Elijah Wright.

51

Effie wants to fly her first class but Solana tells her first class would embarrass her and, anyway, first class is no way to begin anew.

It's not real, she says, life is not first class and so first class is a lie. My whole life has been a lie. Dagmar was a lie

Then let's start in coach, Effie says, I'll sit in back by the toilet for the rest of my life as long as it's with you. I've already bought you Versace. We'll do acupuncture and yoga. We'll do Naxos and Valbonne. We'll bring your mother. We'll live in New York-

Never

-or Miami!

Never. I'll never come back here. Never. No

52

She tells her she's writing two new books: acheiropoieta she's seen from the 8th century and, for reasons she can't quite put her bejeweled fingers upon, accepts as genuine. They elicit a reaction, she says. I'm going to Cacaxtla to see if the same thing happens. That should tell me a lot.

She wonderers if she suffers Cotard delusion or if she's grandiose

Sometimes I wonder if I'm Ulrike Meinhof returned from the grave. Because many years ago, before you were even born, we were close, so close. Nobody *nobody* knows this now except you, everybody's dead, and I will answer no questions, it is part of the secret history of Germany and one of the reasons I live in Switzerland.

Natural and *supernatural* are mutually exclusive, she continues, if I can't reconcile this how can I even be sure I'm alive? They couldn't possibly have created themselves, these miracles, Immaculate Mary gazing up at us from a bowl of Irish stew. Yet something inside us won't let go.

The second is a book on productive hysteria.

It's how playwrights operate, especially homosexuals. I think my grandfather was homosexual. If only he'd written plays instead.

Then you wouldn't have the Stuck, would you?

There are only a few things in life not worth sacrificing.

For instance?

Love. You. I know you've killed someone.

How?

I'm a psychiatrist. I'm only grateful it wasn't me.

53

From the huge Lufthansa Airbus she looks down over the blue Atlantic and then green Europe passing silently below. She drinks cup after little white cup of fine strong Columbian coffee. Our Father Who Art in Heaven, she prays, you fantastic roundabout god of man. I realize that your thoughts are not my thoughts, neither your ways my ways, but this is ridiculous. *Hieronymus bitch and a diaper whore?* Is this the best you can do?

54

Among emergency instructions in the pocket of the seat in front of her Solana also finds a half-used bottle of Elizabeth Arden 5th Avenue perfume, a *Best of Gay Wichita* broadsheet, and a left-behind book from a library at the University of Idaho: Lampe's *The Birth of Hedonism—Cyrenaic Philosophers and Pleasure as a Way of Life.*

Why not *Lies, Passions & Illusions* by François Furet? Seligman's *Possessing Spirits and Healing Selves?* Or even Mclarney's *St. Augustine's Interpretation of the Psalms of Ascent?*

Why here, on this airplane, at this seat, with Solana so receptive and vulnerable?

And why Idaho with its anomalous mascot, the Vandals, a Germanic tribe?

She decides to take the book and read it aloud with Effie. Perhaps together they will discover why it had presented itself so audaciously, so unambiguously.

55

Yes, high above Earth in the heavenly machine Solana closes her eyes and rests, only half comprehending that she is no longer sushi for barbarians, populations glutted on money, useless things. Behind her now the bravura posturing, paralyzing words, blue Octobers. Soon, a forgetting of inessentials, the long-ago meeting in Vărzăreştii Noi significant only in retrospect, the careless cigarette that burns a house

But if not this life, which life? Even now beneath the sundogs of Moldova King Malthus hoists a scepter of despair

Perhaps a tent with bright banners remote upon the steppes of Asia, generous herds beneath a blue and vaulted sky. Or Vegas, baby. Or Consolidated Corrugation Corporation, a clerk beneath dim bulbs. A nurse. Faraway trains. Apache moon. Catholic bells, Orlando timeshares, pregnant strippers, god god god god god god help me

The problem: years of misuse, suspended time, a disappearing future

The miracle: no arrests, pathogen-free. Clean, single

Parsimonious Lord, at least there's that

But O fiery love, amanuensis of my heart, where *can* you be!

56

At the final day Solana's great grandmother had concluded that we are
likely alone in the universe, no god, no
magic, no aliens – our existence less
Epistle of Paul to Romans by Tertius
and more epistle of Chas. Darwin to
Joseph Hooker by his own hand.

In this she took a utopian's joy and com-
fort, a nihilist's casual ease, lamenting
only the undeniable *fact*, the ines-
capable *truth*, that her death was very
near and she would not learn more
about those self-replicating improba-
bly-evolved molecules that likely were
the basis not only of everything we call
life but everything we consider divine.

We should worship *them*, she had whispered to Solona's mother.

Who?

Them, them! she insisted, resolutely
vague.

57

I am descended of Lutherans since Gerhard of Quedlinburg, a brittle family pierced with suicides - and yes, Madame Beria, as you comprehend, the monster sleeps in my blood, too.

For Grandfather was with Jeckeln in Rumbula Forest, a most efficient lieutenant of the Aktion. Years later, Red Army on his doorstep, he murdered five slave-domestics with that very Luger. They had seen too much, his Nazi cohort's black comings and goings.

In extremis I humbled myself before the Lord of Hosts and begged, *implored* His forgiveness. For grandfather, for me, for all those things in my life that must be confronted. Her. You. I begged for your return. Without that, forgiveness didn't matter. I had no choice, there were no options, immanence, transcendence, veracity, *sola fide*, *sola gratia*, the grubby details, false dichotomies - none of this was important anymore. My discontent was lethal: I had become your satellite; you had become my testimony.

O to love in a time when love is still possible, when it has not yet been explained away and destroyed among synaptic equations!

Perhaps we now exist in that brief interval between the old god of Adam and the new god of circuits who may already obtain, Horologist of infinite will and power.

What will we call this new god? GOD, of course: *Nations will come to your light, And kings to the brightness of your rising*!

Nonetheless, everything still takes forever. Isn't that interesting?

Suddenly on German television a Russian woman arrested for trafficking in Munich. When the reporter mentioned the Călărași District in Moldova, God exploded in my heart. I knew! I *knew*!

Four weeks later I found your Salvationist mother who had all but become your martyr.

Finding her wouldn't have been so dif-
ficult if only I had asked your name

Endnotes

1 $N = R_* \cdot f_p \cdot n_e \cdot f_l \cdot f_c \cdot L$

where:

N = the number of <u>civilizations</u> in our galaxy with which radio-communication might be possible (i.e. which are on our current past <u>light cone</u>);

and

R_* = the average rate of <u>star formation</u> in <u>our galaxy</u>

f_p = the fraction of those stars that have <u>planets</u>

n_e = the average number of planets that can potentially support <u>life</u> per star that has planets

f_l = the fraction of planets that could support life that actually develop life at some point

f_i = the fraction of planets with life that actually go on to develop <u>intelligent</u> life (civilizations)

f_c = the fraction of civilizations that develop a technology that releases detectable signs of their existence into space

L = the length of time for which such civilizations release detectable signals into space[8]

(http://en.wikipedia.org/wiki/Drake_equation)

Ch. 11 *The Nutty Professor*

Ch. 23 Jerry Reed, *Eastbound and Down*

Ch. 48 Cypress Hill, *Black Sunday*

About the author

pd mallamo has appeared in a wide range of international literary journals including *Barcelona Review*, *Granta* and *Conte*. He is a MacDowell Colony fellow and has degrees from BYU and the University of Kansas.

www.ingramcontent.com/pod-product-compliance
Lightning Source LLC
Chambersburg PA
CBHW072034170626
46811CB00008B/3070